This book belongs to:

Finn, cockrell

Bright Sparks books have been created
with the help of experts in early childhood education.
They are designed to help young children achieve
success in their early learning years.

Retold by Sue Graves
Illustrated by Gaby Hansen

Reading consultants: Betty Root and Monica Hughes

This is a Parragon Publishing book
First published 2006

Parragon Publishing
Queen Street House
4 Queen Street
Bath BA1 1HE, UK

ISBN 1-40547-965-5
Printed in China

The Three Little Pigs

p

Helping your child read

Bright Sparks readers are closely linked to recognized learning strategies. Their vocabulary has been carefully selected from word lists recommended by educational experts.

Read the story

Read the story
to your child
a few times.

The three little pigs were happy i
their houses.
Then one day they saw a big ba
He wanted to eat them.
So the three little pigs ran away
the big bad wolf.
They ran into their houses.

16

Follow your finger

Run your finger under
the text as you read.
Soon your child will begin to
follow the words with you.

Look at the pictures

Talk about the pictures. They will help your child understand the story.

The three little pigs ran away from the big bad wolf.

17

Give it a try

Let your child try reading the large type on each right-hand page. It repeats a line from the story.

Join in

When your child is ready, encourage him or her to join in with the main story text. Shared reading is the first step to reading alone.

Once upon a time there were three little pigs.
The three little pigs lived with their mommy.
One day she said, “This house is too small.”
So the three little pigs set off to make new houses.

There were three little pigs.

The first little pig met a girl with some straw.
"I will make a house of straw," said the first little pig.

So the first little pig did just that.
His house had walls of straw and a roof of straw.

“I will make a house of straw.”

The second little pig met a boy with some sticks.
"I will make a house of sticks," said the second little pig.

So the second little pig did just that. His house had walls of sticks and a roof of sticks.

“I will make a house of sticks.”

The third little pig met a man with some bricks.
"I will make a house of bricks," said the third little pig.

So the third little pig did just that. Her house had walls of bricks, a chimney of bricks, and a roof of bricks.

“I will make a house of bricks.”

The three little pigs were happy in
their houses.
Then one day they saw a big bad wolf.
He wanted to eat them.
So the three little pigs ran away from
the big bad wolf.
They ran into their houses.

The three little pigs ran away from the big bad wolf.

The big bad wolf went to the house of straw.
"Little pig, let me come in," he cried.
But the first little pig said, "Go away!"

So the big bad wolf huffed and puffed.
And he blew the house down.

The big bad wolf huffed and puffed.

Then the big bad wolf went to the house of sticks.
"Little pig, let me come in," he cried.
But the second little pig said, "Go away!"

So the big bad wolf huffed and puffed, and huffed and puffed.
And he blew the house down.

The big bad wolf huffed and puffed.

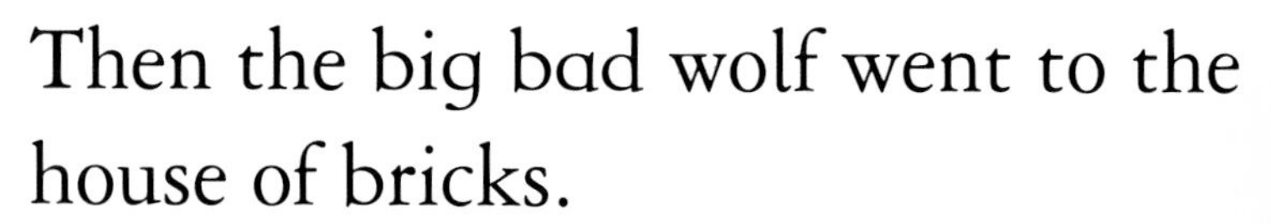

Then the big bad wolf went to the house of bricks.
"Little pig, let me come in," he cried.
But the three little pigs said,
"Go away! Go away! Go away!"
So the big bad wolf huffed and puffed, and huffed and puffed.

"Go away! Go away! Go away!"

He huffed and he puffed, and he
huffed and he puffed.
But still the house did not fall down.

Then the big bad wolf went onto
the roof.
"I will go down the chimney," he said.

“I will go down the chimney.”

So the three little pigs got a big pot of water.
They put the big pot of water on the fire.
When he came down the chimney, the wolf fell into the hot water.
And that was the end of him!

The wolf fell into the hot water.

Look back in your book.

Can you read these words?

Can you answer these questions?

Which little pig made a house of straw?

Who wanted to eat the three little pigs?

What happened when the wolf went down the chimney?

The End